For Mom, who taught me to play

A NOTE FROM THE ARTIST

The digital paintings for this book were made using Procreate with scanned digital textures. I chose this medium to infuse the art with energy and movement, and was influenced by the work of Italian Futurists who praised invention, modernity, speed, and disruption, with a specific focus on the modern urban scene.

This book has taken many years to envision, and our global community has been through a lot of difficult change during that time. *Jump In!* is not just a story for me, it is the philosophy that guides how I live my life—full of joy, play, and love of community!

I'd like to give a special shout out to the Baltimore jump rope team, Jump For Joy!, and the Double Dutch Holiday Classic participants at the Apollo Theater. And to my amazing agent, Lori Nowicki, for pulling this from my personal slush pile. It's time to Jump In!

BLOOMSBURY CHILDREN'S BOOKS
Bloomsbury Publishing Inc., part of Bloomsbury Publishing Plc
1385 Broadway, New York, NY 10018

BLOOMSBURY, BLOOMSBURY CHILDREN'S BOOKS, and the Diana logo
are trademarks of Bloomsbury Publishing Plc

First published in the United States of America in January 2023
by Bloomsbury Children's Books

Copyright © 2023 by Shadra Strickland

Bloomsbury books may be purchased for business or promotional use. For information on bulk purchases please contact Macmillan Corporate and Premium Sales Department at specialmarkets@macmillan.com

Library of Congress Cataloging-in-Publication Data
available upon request
ISBN 978-1-61963-580-7 (hardcover)
ISBN 978-1-5476-0315-2 (e-book) · ISBN 978-1-5476-0316-9 (e-PDF)

Typeset in Burlesk, Jost, and Londrina · Book design by John Candell
Printed and bound in China by Leo Paper Products, Heshan, Guangdong
1 2 3 4 5 6 7 8 9 10

To find out more about our authors and books visit www.bloomsbury.com and sign up for our newsletters.

JUMP IN!

SHADRA STRICKLAND

BLOOMSBURY
CHILDREN'S BOOKS
NEW YORK   LONDON   OXFORD   NEW DELHI   SYDNEY

Asphalt sizzles in wait,
ropes lie in the corner as bait.
Tic tac, tic tac through the wind.
Feet bounce up the block in time . . .

Grab two ropes. Make a loop.
Everyone line up. Jump through the hoop!

Two becomes four. Four more is eight.
Rock back-and-forth. Don't hesitate.

First ones up, the Delancy twins.
Double Dutch divas, go girls . . .

Jump
in!

Sisters of the sidewalk, we jump in twos,
clapping our hands to the Double Dutch blues.
Jump over, jump under, spin 'round, and then,
Hey, Leroy, we see you, come on . . .

Jump
in!

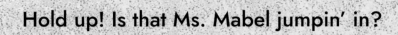

Hold up! Is that Ms. Mabel jumpin' in?

Slide over, Keisha.
Hold this, Soo.
Leroy Jones gon' show you what to do.
Spring off the ground,
then backwards, and bend—

I burn it up with a ball and a net,
but I got moves you ain't seen yet.
You'll squeal and blush with the heat I bring,
my hip-hop tricks will make you sing.

Get back youngstas,
I know how it's done.
Been the queen of hopscotch since I was one.
Hold my purse before I begin,
didn't think an ol' lady still had the skins?

I could teach you a few things about jumpin' in!

Is there a doctor in the house just in case
her legs give out from under her waist?

**Be nice,
everybody . . .**

My arms are getting tired, I can't turn no mo'.

See Ms. Mabel with that funky wiggle!
She sure knows how to make it jiggle.
Just how long do you think she'll go?

Keep turning, Gwen!

What a glorious day, Reverend, do preachers jump in?

Let us rejoice in the good word,
keep your hearts as light as a bird.
Give the man upstairs his due time,
live a life that's good and fine.

From the birds of the air to the fish in the sea,
this Earth was made for you and me.
Love your neighbor and let's all say "Amen,"
there's room for us all, come on . . .

My turn at last!
Been waitin' all day
to put these schoolbooks down and play.
Studied hard, did my homework, and then
Mama finally let me out to jump in!

Been practicing my moves all week,
watch this skateboard spin to the beat.

It's much more fun when there are friends,
make room everybody, cuz I'm comin' in!

Breathe!

Touch the ground!

Leap!

Now turn the rope faster,
speed's the game.
Our feet will burn it up,
like wheels on a train.

Spin!

Around the world
and side to side, c'mon!

Did that streetlight flicker?
Did my mom just shout?
It's been fun jumping in but it's time to . . .